Princess Cupcake Jones

Won't Go To School!

By Ylleya Fields

Illustrated by Michael LaDuca

Belle Publishing · Cleveland, Ohio

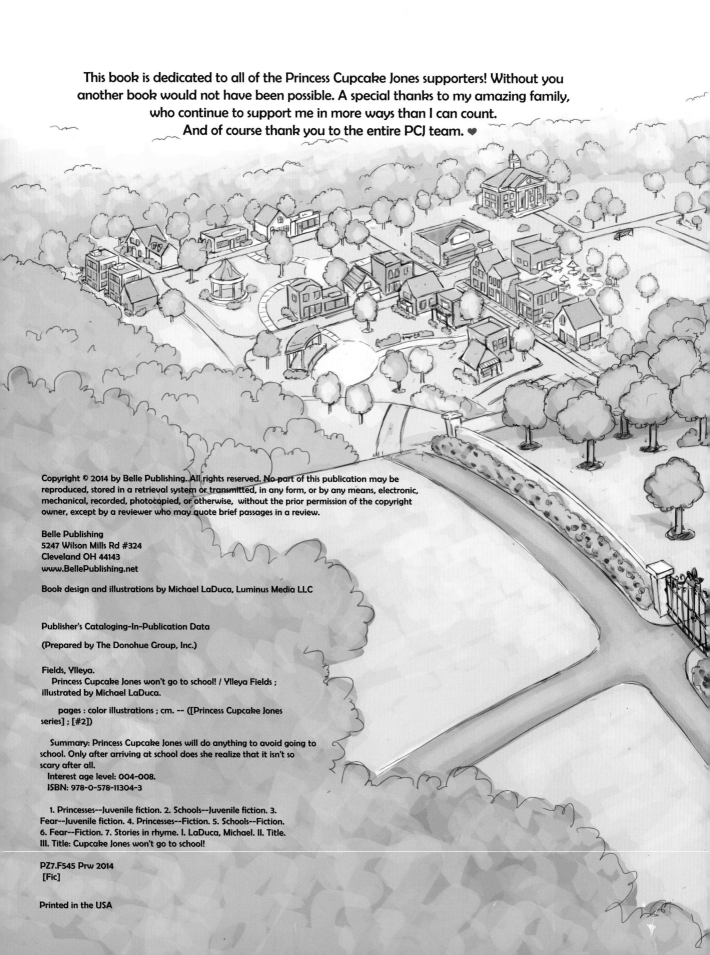

This book is dedicated to all of the Princess Cupcake Jones supporters! Without you another book would not have been possible. A special thanks to my amazing family, who continue to support me in more ways than I can count.
And of course thank you to the entire PCJ team. ❤

Belle Publishing
5247 Wilson Mills Rd #324
Cleveland OH 44143
www.BellePublishing.net

Book design and illustrations by Michael LaDuca, Luminus Media LLC

Publisher's Cataloging-In-Publication Data

(Prepared by The Donohue Group, Inc.)

Fields, Ylleya.
    Princess Cupcake Jones won't go to school! / Ylleya Fields ;
illustrated by Michael LaDuca.

    pages : color illustrations ; cm. -- ([Princess Cupcake Jones
series] ; [#2])

    Summary: Princess Cupcake Jones will do anything to avoid going to
school. Only after arriving at school does she realize that it isn't so
scary after all.
    Interest age level: 004-008.
    ISBN: 978-0-578-11304-3

    1. Princesses--Juvenile fiction. 2. Schools--Juvenile fiction. 3.
Fear--Juvenile fiction. 4. Princesses--Fiction. 5. Schools--Fiction.
6. Fear--Fiction. 7. Stories in rhyme. I. LaDuca, Michael. II. Title.
III. Title: Cupcake Jones won't go to school!

PZ7.F545 Prw 2014
[Fic]

Printed in the USA

The end of the summer was finally here,
which meant, in the kingdom, a brand new school year.

But at 6 Garden Place, Cupcake sullenly pouted.

"I won't go to school! No, I won't!" Cupcake shouted.

The Queen watched from the doorway, perplexed as to why.
"But you were excited," was her calm reply.

"I'm not!" Cupcake said. Her foot stomped with a boom.
"I don't want to go. I'm not leaving this room!"

"Well," said the Queen, "I'm sorry you feel that way.
Today, my dear, is your official first day."
"Not today!" Cupcake moaned. She had to think quick!
I know, Cupcake thought, I'll pretend that I'm sick.

Cupcake let out a cough,

then started to sneeze.

She thought to herself, faking sick is a breeze.

"Mommy, I'm sick!" Cupcake said with a yell.
"Oh dear. . .," said the Queen. "You're not feeling too well?"

"I'll make an appointment with the doctor today.
He'll have medicine to fix you up right away.
The meds might taste yucky. You may need a shot.
But we don't want you to keep any germs that you've got."

"I'm better already. My forehead feels cool!"
What would Cupcake do next to get out of school?

"Hurry!" Mom said. "It's time to get dressed."
Then Cupcake remembered, "My tutu's a mess.
I can't go to school in anything less!
No, I can't go to school. I can't take the stress!"

"No worries, my dear, I washed it last night.
I knew that you'd want that tutu just right."

Desperate, she thought of one final plan.
If this didn't work, who knows what else can!

"When it's time to go, I'll hide instead.
No one will find me under my bed."

The Queen called out, "Are you ready to go?"
There wasn't an answer—not a yes or a no.

"Where are you? We're leaving," her mother said.
Then the Queen saw two feet sticking out from the bed.

"Mommy, I'm scared. What if I don't like school?
What if no one likes me? Or my tutu's not cool?"

The Queen hugged Cupcake tightly and said,
"Don't worry about that." She patted her head.

21

"A new place can seem quite scary, it's true.
Don't let fear stop you from doing something new."

23

When Cupcake Jones arrived in her class,
she was greeted warmly by her teacher, Ms.Bass.

Ms. Bass seemed nice. Not the least bit too scary.
Still Cupcake glanced around ever so wary.

Cupcake heard a voice. "I like your tutu.
It looks just like mine, except mine is blue."

"I'm Violet! What's your name?" the little girl said.
"I'm Cupcake," said the princess, with a tilt of her head.

Violet asked the princess, "Would you like to play?"
Cupcake had a new friend—on her very first day!

Cupcake turned to the Queen and hugged her goodbye.
And whispered in her ear, "I'll give school a try."

Hand-in-hand with Violet, they ran off to explore.
Cupcake Jones was not afraid of school anymore!

KOHLBERLIN ACADEMY
Kindergarten - Ms. Bass